To the Sacramento
Public Library—
be grateful!
Shelly Be...

Thank You, God

Holly Bea

Illustrated by Kim Howard

H J Kramer
Starseed Press
Tiburon, California

Art Director: Linda Kramer
Design and production: Jan Phillips, San Anselmo, California

Library of Congress Cataloging-in-Publication Data

Bea, Holly, 1956-
    Thank you, God / Holly Bea ; illustrated by Kim Howard.
    p. cm.
Summary: As a young girl goes through her day, she continually finds
things for which to be grateful and sees that thanking God can chase her
cares away.
    [1. Prayers—Fiction. 2. Gratitude—Fiction. 3. Stories in rhyme.] I.
Howard, Kim, ill. II. Title.
PZ8.3.B3485Th 2003
[E]—dc21

                                                    2002155300

H J Kramer
Starseed Press
P.O. Box 1082
Tiburon, California 94920

Printed in Singapore

10 9 8 7 6 5 4 3 2 1

Thank you, God, for giving me
the best brother in the
whole world.
H. B.

For Garrett, my lifelong friend.
Thank you.
K. H.

When I wake up each morning,
The first thing that I say,
Is thank you, God, for everything,
And for this brand new day.

Thank you, God, for where I live,
It's more than just a house.
It's filled with love from God above,
And an itty-bitty mouse.

Thanks for our kitchen table,
We always gather there,
To start the day with breakfast,
And an early morning prayer.

I'm thankful for the yellow bus,
That takes me to my school.
I'm grateful for the teachers there,
Who teach the Golden Rule.

GRASS

And when I'm feeling sad and blue,
There's just one thing to say.
Thank you, God, is all it takes,
To chase my cares away.

Thanks for my best friend, Megan,
She's smart and very funny.
She wrinkles up her nose and then,
Pretends that she's a bunny.

God, thank you for my brother,
You know he's such a tease.
He kind of makes me crazy,
But he watches out for me.

Thank you for the jungle gym,
I like to climb up high.
Megan's thankful for the swings,
'Cause her toes can touch the sky.

There's someone else I'm thankful for,
Miss Judy lives next door.
She's always got a smile for me,
And gingersnaps galore!

Thank you, God, for Daddy,
He's big and tall and strong.
He tickles me and makes me laugh,
And keeps me safe from harm.

I'm thankful for my mommy,
She guides me on my way.
She talks to you, I'm sure she does,
And knows just what to say.

Thank you, God, for Nana,
And all her squishy hugs.
Thank you for my grandpa,
And his best friend, Mr. Pug.

I can't forget my turtle, Gus,
I'm thankful for him, too.
He's kind of shy and quiet,
But he's steady and he's true.

Thanks for the bed I sleep in,
When Mom turns out the lights.
There's a warm and cozy blanket,
And sweet dreams to fill my nights.

Tonight I'll count my blessings,
I'm thankful for each one.
Then close my eyes and go to sleep,
Until tomorrow comes.